Frog

Pictures by Pauline Baynes

Helen Piers

and Water Shrew

Kestrel Books

KESTREL BOOKS

Published by Penguin Books Ltd
Harmondsworth, Middlesex, England

First published in 1981

ISBN 0 7226 5731 5
Filmset by Northumberland Press Ltd,
Gateshead, Tyne and Wear
Printed in Great Britain by
Fakenham Press Ltd
Fakenham, Norfolk

Water Shrew squeezed out of her cool damp hole and ran down the bank to the pond. Outside it was another scorching hot day. She wriggled her nose anxiously up towards the sky.

"And still no rain," she squeaked.

"Perfect! Another scorching hot day! Perfect!" Frog was basking in the sun. Drowsily he watched the dragonflies darting about over his head until he began to feel a bit uncomfortably hot.

"Ah, ready to cool off now!" he croaked, and he flopped lazily into the pond.

Down at the bottom Water Shrew
was scurrying busily in and out of the
reeds. Frog watched her catch and eat two
beetles, a spider, three worms and a
stickleback.

"And she'll soon be back for more!" he
croaked.

In a few minutes Frog was feeling
uncomfortably chilly. He swam to the
bank, clambered out, and stretched
himself in the sun.

"Perfect!" he croaked, as he began to
warm up again. "Perfect!"

Water Shrew was back in her hole, trying to get some sleep before it was time to go out again. Soon she'd need some more to eat. *She* didn't have time to lie in the sun and splash about in the water all day like a frog.

"I might get off to sleep," she squeaked irritably, poking her nose out of her hole, "if he'd stop croaking."

It was a very hot summer. Every day the sun blazed down out of a clear blue sky, and it didn't rain at all.

Then one day, when Frog flopped into the water, it only came up to his neck. Two young newts were splashing by. "The pond's drying up," one of them croaked. "We're going to live in the stream."

"No need to go dashing off yet," Frog croaked after them lazily. "It'll rain soon."

But next day Frog flopped into the pond and found himself sitting in a muddy puddle. He was squatting there, trying to cool off, when suddenly he flung himself flat as a pancake into the mud.

"Help!" he croaked. "There's no water to hide under!" A kingfisher had perched above his head.

Luckily the kingfisher wasn't hungry, but when at last it flew away, Frog had decided it was time now to be off to the stream.

But oh dear, he didn't know the way.

Then Frog saw Water Shrew pattering about on the hard mud, searching in the cracks for any food that might be left behind.

"Ah, *she'll* be going to the stream," he croaked. "I'll get there by following her."

But at that moment Water Shrew was keeping an eye on Frog. She wanted to go to the stream too, but *she* didn't know how to get there either.

"I'll follow him," she squeaked. "He's sure to be going."

Meanwhile Frog was getting too hot, so he hopped away to find some shade.

"He's going *now*!" Water Shrew squealed. She scurried back to her hole, and after a lot of squeaking and bustle tumbled out again, followed by four baby water shrews.

"Oh dear!" she sighed, when she saw her children out in the daylight. "You're not nearly old enough to leave the nest." Then she looked at what was left of the pond, and her nose wrinkled up sadly.

"Come along," she said.

Frog saw Water Shrew hurry past. She was really making for a clump of grass, where she'd decided to hide until Frog went on again.

But, "She's going to the stream!" Frog thought. Then he saw the baby shrews.

"What! Children too!" he croaked, hopping along after them. He wasn't used to having children around.

So Frog and Water Shrew set off to find the stream together. Neither knew the way, but both thought the other one did.

At first Water Shrew thought Frog would never get going. Then, without warning, he suddenly jumped.

"He's going!" she squeaked. "Come along!" By the time she'd gathered up her children, Frog had disappeared into a wheatfield. Water Shrew thought she'd never find him in the forest of tall dry stalks. Then at last she heard him croaking, and there he was – basking in a patch of sunshine.

"Thank goodness!" she sighed.

Of course, Frog wasn't going anywhere. He was only warming up while he waited to follow Water Shrew to the stream.

"She's off at last!" he croaked to
himself. Water Shrew was hurrying away.
When he caught up with her, there she
was – gobbling down a beetle.

And so it went on all day. When Water
Shrew scurried off to find something to

eat, Frog always followed her. And when
Frog jumped away to find some sun Water
Shrew would follow *him*. Water Shrew
found it hard keeping up with Frog. He
jumped so haphazardly that she never
knew where he was going to land next.

At last in the evening Frog jumped and happened to land outside the wheatfield. At once Water Shrew and her children ran past him, and hid.

"Good!" Frog croaked. "She's come out of that dry stuffy place at last."

Neither of them wanted to go further that day. Frog caught some flies for his supper, and then snuggled in among the dead leaves. Water Shrew badly wanted some soft damp soil, in which to dig a hole, but the ground was dry and hard everywhere. She had to settle her children down for the night under a dandelion, as comfortably as possible.

During the night Water Shrew woke up suddenly, feeling homesick. She could smell something and she couldn't help running out to see what it was. Not far away she found a mound of soft damp soil.

Water Shrew began to dig happily – a short narrow passage, widening out at the end – when all of a sudden the soil gave way under her. She felt herself dropping head first down and down until she landed with a thud in a wide dark tunnel.

Water Shrew only had time to grab a fat worm, which had fallen in with her, when a hot wind blew down the tunnel, towards her. She heard a rumbling echoing noise, which was getting nearer quickly. Then she rolled up tightly and tucked her head well in, because she was being pushed, pummelled, scratched and kicked.

"This must be the end of me!" she squealed, as she was thrown bodily out into the open air. But she held on tight to the worm.

It was the middle of the night when
Frog woke to find that Water Shrew
wasn't under the dandelion leaves. He
took a few hops here and there –
haphazardly, to see if he could find her.

His third hop landed him in front of a
small hillock just in time to see it explode
into a shower of soil and pebbles, as Water
Shrew hurtled out, somersaulted in the
air, and landed on the grass. A mole's long

pink snout and spade-like paws appeared in the pile of soil for a moment, and then disappeared.

"Well! If she messes about like this," Frog croaked, "we'll never get to the stream."

Water Shrew was very bruised and shaken, but she wasn't badly hurt.

She was feeling much better by the early morning when Frog really did seem to be on his way to the stream.

He was easy to follow this morning.
He didn't jump about haphazardly, and
he didn't stop to bask in the sun. He just
hopped on and on in a straight line, as if
he was in a hurry to get somewhere.

Water Shrew followed him through
dusty dry grass, up and down hillocks, in
and out of gravelly ruts and hollows, and
over rocks which had got burning hot in
the sun. She was helping her children
through a prickly hedge, when she heard a
loud splash, and then Frog croaking,
"Perfect! Perfect!"

"Frog is in the stream!" she squeaked.
"Hurry! We're there!"

She found Frog sitting in a watering can! "Nothing to eat in there!" she squeaked sharply. "That's not the stream."

Frog was croaking contentedly. This morning he'd suddenly got a feeling in his legs that there was water over here on the other side of the field. He'd been so parched that he'd hopped over at once to find it, forgetting all about Water Shrew.

"Goodness!" he croaked, when he saw her. "She'll go to the stream without me." But try as he would, Frog couldn't get out of that watering can. There he had to stay until the evening, when by good luck somebody upset it.

Water Shrew was very disappointed in Frog.

"Why does he waste time like this?" she thought. She ran off then to find something to eat. Soon she was feeling better-tempered – they were in a garden, and there was *damp* soil, *green* grass, plenty to eat, and in places it was *raining*.

In the evening, Frog found her settled comfortably in a cosy hole in a bank.

They stayed for several days in the garden. Frog never thought about going to the stream now – he had rain to get soaked in here, and the food was delicious. But Water Shrew fretted to be off. It *was* comfortable in the garden, but she didn't feel really at home. Also she wanted to see her children swim like other water shrews.

It was Frog who – by mistake – made it quite impossible for Water Shrew to stay in the garden any longer. He had had that feeling in his legs again – there was water somewhere and he'd got to find it! Water Shrew had followed him up onto some very hard ground.

"Oh, he's really found the stream this time," she squealed, when she heard a big splash. Frog *had* found some water. But he hadn't croaked contentedly as it closed over his head – the water was soapy and very hot! He had jumped out at once *plunk* on to dry land, and then, "Thank goodness!" Frog croaked, as SPLASH! he'd landed in a soothingly cool "puddle".

"Watch out!"

Water Shrew dashed helter-skelter out of the way – a pair of large green eyes was looking at Frog!

The first Frog knew of any danger was a big furry paw with long sharp claws lifted above his head. He jumped. The paw splashed into the "puddle". He jumped again, and he heard the claws scrape the ground where he'd been sitting. Then he jumped again, landing beside Water Shrew.

"Watch out!" he croaked cheerfully, as he took a last big leap and disappeared into a flowerbed – the green eyes were there again. This time they were looking at Water Shrew!

She felt a claw miss her by a whisker, as she took to her heels back to her hole in the bank. There she was safe, but for a long time whenever she peeped out, she saw the green eyes watching her.

After that Water Shrew had no peace. She never knew when she'd find a large paw just behind her, or see two green eyes staring into her hole. In the end she was too frightened to go out at all, and she and her children got so hungry that they felt quite raw and rasping inside.

One night Water Shrew slipped quietly out of her hole and scurried past the watering can and through the prickly hedge with her children scampering behind her.

She had forgotten how dry and dusty it was out in the field. But she scurried on, calling to her children not to lag behind. That night she didn't care where they went, as long as they got far away from the garden and that big cat.

They went on and on, until their feet were sore with running on the hard ground. After a while they began to hear weird creaking noises coming out of the dark above their heads, and sudden scufflings near them on the ground. An eerie "To-whoo! To-whoo!" came first from one place above them, and then another. Water Shrew shivered every time she heard it.

Worst of all, wherever they ran she kept hearing a soft *plunk* as if somebody was landing on the ground behind them.

"Come on! We're being followed!" she panted, as they ran round and round in circles, trying to get out of that frightening place.

Suddenly Water Shrew stopped and wriggled her nose up into the air. What was that smell? It was like a mixture of stickleback, dragonfly, water weed and other smells she'd nearly forgotten. Whatever could it be?

Just then, there was another *plunk* – very close behind them this time – and before Water Shrew could stop them, her children were running towards it, squealing at the tops of their voices.

She found them happily running round Frog, who was croaking cheerfully as if he was pleased to see them. He looked thin and dusty.

Water Shrew wondered why Frog had
been following them. Perhaps she'd made
a mistake, and he didn't really know the
way to —

"Oh! The stream!" she squeaked
suddenly. "That smell is the stream!"
"Ah, the stream at last!" Frog croaked.
"Yes, I can feel it in my legs."

Water Shrew didn't see the owl coming. But Frog's eyes were on top of his head. He saw an enormous shadow, black against the sky, gliding silently but swiftly towards Water Shrew.

"Get going! Get going!" he croaked. Then he jumped – straight towards the owl. The owl swerved, not knowing whether to grab the furry little animal or the bright green one, which had suddenly jumped almost into its claws . . .

Water Shrew scurried away with her children close under her tail, only stopping to sniff the air to make sure they were going the right way, or to listen for a *plunk* behind them.

"He'll be all right," she kept telling her children. "Frog jumps so haphazardly. Nobody will catch Frog."

It was just getting light when they came to some long grass.

"Listen!" Water Shrew squeaked. They could hear a gurgling, chattering watery sound which never stopped. "That's the stream!"

The little water shrews were still enjoying their first swim when they heard a big splash. Slowly and thankfully Frog sank into the stream.

"Perfect!" he croaked. "Perfect!"

The little shrews swam round and round Frog as he sat at the bottom and soaked up the water. "It's this feeling I get in my legs," he was croaking. "That's how we found our way to the stream."

Water Shrew couldn't help wrinkling her nose crossly when she heard him.

"Why *did* I waste all that time following Frog," she squeaked to herself. "He didn't know the way any more than I did." But then she shivered. She'd remembered that eerie "To-whoo! To-whoo!"

Without Frog she would never have got to the stream at all.

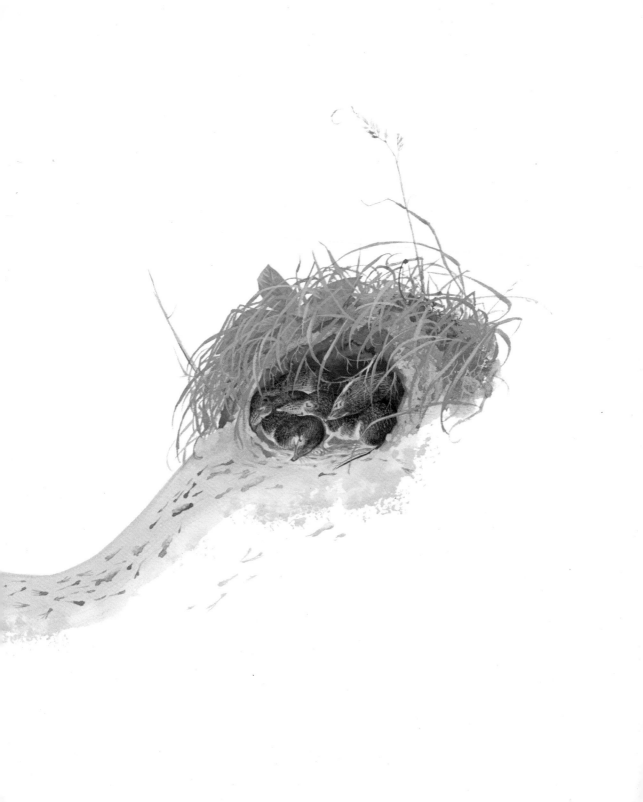